CHAPTER 1

After the Storm

A powerful **storm** hit a small island off the coast of Florida.

The next morning, Rico went down to the beach.

He was hunting for anything strange or rare.

Rico often found objects that had washed up on shore after a storm.

When he found something, Rico would take it to a scientist in town named Dr Agon.

* $ $ *

Dr Agon paid Rico for finding things.

That morning, Rico saw a pile of *glowing* objects lying on the sand.

They looked like giant **eggs**.

Rico also saw a young man.

The young man was **burying** the eggs in the sand.

CHAPTER 2
The Eggs

Rico hid and watched the young man.

"Why is he burying them?" wondered Rico.

He knew Dr Agon would pay him a lot for one of those **eggs.**

When the eggs were all buried,

the young man hurried away.

Rico stepped carefully across the sand.

He picked out a spot and then began to dig with his hands.

Soon, he had dug up one of the **strange eggs**.

Rico picked it up.

He felt something moving inside the egg.

Rico **yelled**. The egg tipped over
in his hands.

Something inside the egg was **alive**.

Rico tucked the egg under his arm and rushed away from the beach.

Dr Agon would be glad to see his new discovery.

CHAPTER 3
Dr Agon

Rico hurried to the doctor's office.

"What did you bring me this time, Rico?" asked the doctor.

"I'm not sure," said Rico. "It was on the beach."

The doctor examined the egg
carefully.

"I think there is something inside," said Rico.

Dr Agon felt the **smooth** surface of the egg.

He had never seen anything like it before.

"There are **lots** more on the beach," said Rico.

A strange smile passed across the doctor's face. "Where are they?" he asked.

"They are buried in the sand," said Rico. "They are next to the place with all the *white* stones."

Dr Agon pulled out a handful of money and shoved it at Rico.

Then he grabbed Rico's shoulder and shook him.

"Don't tell anyone else what you found," said the doctor.

Rico nodded his head, frightened. Then he ran out of the office.

CHAPTER 4

Terror On the Beach

*T*hat night, a *full moon* shone down on the beach.

Dr Agon stepped out from the shadow of some palm trees.

He was carrying a shovel.

"If there are more of those eggs," he said, "they will be worth a **fortune**."

The doctor walked across the
sand.

He found the spot where Rico
had dug up the first egg.

Moments later, Dr Agon had dug
up another egg.

He held it in his hands. It
glowed in the *moonlight*.

"I'm going to be rich!" he told
himself.

Then the shell began to move.

Tiny teeth poked through a

crack.

"Ouch!" Dr Agon yelled and dropped the egg.

Something had **bitten** him.

Then, all around him, the sand began to move.

Dark things began to poke out of the sand. He saw tiny wings and claws and sharp, little teeth.

Soon the beach was covered with dark, hissing creatures.

"At last!" cried the doctor. "I knew they were real!"

The creatures were **dragons**.

And they were hungry.

The next morning, Rico returned
to the beach.

He was hunting for more strange
objects.

All he found was a white hat.

Of Dragons and Near-Dragons

If dragons did exist and really laid eggs, they would probably lay them in the same ways their reptile cousins do. Most reptiles dig a hole in soft dirt or sand, drop their eggs into the hole, and then cover them up.

Reptiles do not produce their own body heat. They cannot sit on their eggs and keep them warm like birds do. So reptiles depend on sunlight and the warm ground to help hatch their eggs.

Female pythons sometimes curl their long bodies around a group of eggs. If it gets too cold, the pythons shiver to make their blood circulate faster and warm up. This helps to warm up the eggs too.

Sea turtles return to the same beaches year after year to lay their eggs. Some sea turtles form bands of thousands of females. They climb the beaches together and lay their eggs in the middle of the night.

Reptiles can lay as many as 200 eggs at one time!

On one stretch of beach in Florida, more than 68,100 kilograms (67 tons) of sea turtle eggs are laid each year.

Leatherback turtles travel across the ocean to reach their egg-laying beaches. One leatherback tracked by scientists swam more than 19,000 kilometres (12,000 miles)!

ABOUT THE AUTHOR

Michael Dahl is the author of more than 200 books for children and young adults. He has won the AEP Distinguished Achievement Award three times for his non-fiction. His *Finnegan Zwake* mystery series was shortlisted twice by the Anthony and Agatha awards. He has also written the *Library of Doom* series. He is a featured speaker at conferences around the country on graphic novels and high-interest books for boys.

ABOUT THE ILLUSTRATOR

Richard Pellegrino is a professional illustrator. His work has been published by CMYK, Night Shade Books, Compass Press, and Tale Bones Press. He is also an accomplished figurative painter and has shown his oil paintings in numerous galleries.

GLOSSARY

allies people or countries that give support to each other

creature living thing that is human or animal

examined looked carefully at something

frightened scared

rare special or not common

rule have power over something

surface outside or outermost layer of something

terror great fear

DISCUSSION QUESTIONS

1. Rico liked to search for treasure. Would you want to be a treasure hunter? Why or why not?

2. Was it right for Rico to take one of the eggs? Explain your answer.

3. Did you know that dragons were in the eggs? If not, what did you think was in the eggs? If so, how did you guess?

WRITING PROMPTS

1. Rico sees a young man burying the eggs on the beach. Who do you think the young man was? Write a paragraph describing him and who he works for.

2. Do you think Dr Agon was evil or just greedy? Write a paragraph explaining your answer.

3. Were you surprised by the ending of this story? Why or why not? What do you think happened to Dr Agon?

MORE BOOKS TO READ

LIBRARY OF DOOM

Meet the mysterious Librarian. Keeper of the world's most dangerous books, sworn enemy of monsters made of paper and ink, crusader of young people threatened by ancient curses... Enter the Library of Doom to follow these heart-pounding adventures.